joyohboy
raising peaceful kids

"My Mindful Book of ABCs" is part of a series of books inspiring children.
©2016 Kathy Walsh, Joyohboy. All rights reserved. Printed in the U.S.A. First Edition
Book design by Anne Yonkers

It's time for my ABCs

Let's go,
Let's fly,
Let's dream today.

Let's go on a magic carpet ride.
Let's go down the ABC slide.

A is for amazing,
that is what I am.

B is for beautiful
that's what I see in you.

C is for caring
for all animals on the earth.

D is for doing
fun things today.

E is for excellence
in all I do.

F is for fantastic,
that's what I am.

G is for grateful,
for all things in my life.

H is for happy,
I want you happy too!

I is for inner wisdom,
I seek.

J is for jumping
with joy today.

K is for kindness
for you and me.

L is for love,
love is all that I see.

M is for me,
being all I can be.

N is for nature,
that I play in today.

O is for Oh!
What a beautiful day!

P is for please,
in all that I ask.

Q is for quiet,
when I go within.

R is for restful,
as I connect with peace

S is for seeing the light in you.

T is for truth that I speak every day.

U is for under
the trees we play.

V is very,
very happy today.

W is wondering
where my imagination will go

X is for xylophone,
playing sweet music for me.

Y is for yellow,
the color of sunshine I see.

Z is for zen,
how I feel today.

As I go out and play,
on my magic carpet ride,
going down the ABC slide.

Photograph by Neil Roberts

CLARE WASSERMANN, Illustrator

Clare Wassermann hails from the very middle of England and has been painting and sketching since childhood, but more recently has worked in acrylic and oils on a larger scale. She loves the idea of layer upon layer in paint and collage evoking memories and experiences. Some paintings have ten or even twenty layers built up and most are in response to her meditation and yoga practice. All are a pure celebration of her external and internal landscapes.

Juxtaposition of edges and colour combinations excite her. Sometimes she works in fabric and stitch for even more texture. Clare uses her intuition, as far as possible, to take her on the journey towards a final balance point. This art practice becomes a metaphor for life. This is the third book in the Joyohboy series that Clare has illustrated. Others include *My Mindful Book of ABCs* and *Today an Elephant I Will Be*.

www.clarewassermannart.com

praise for joyohboy
raising peaceful kids

"I was completely captured by Kathy's quest for mindfulness after learning about her book - **30 Days to a Mindful Home**. After all, I am a mom of three who works from home and practically lives in chaos. It was almost as if this book at FOUND me in my darkest hour."

~ Vera, *Audrey & Vera, The Hustle Diaries*

"As any parent who gets interrupted 17 times a minute can appreciate, the author sprinkles reviews and helpful tools for applying her peaceful parenting tips. Today, my daughter and I are applying Kathy's tools for encouraging kids to self-regulate emotions. When children learn to manage their emotions, they can increase their emotional intelligence, boost their confidence, increase brain function, improve their social skills, and value peace. According to **Raising Peaceful Kids**: peaceful parents, peaceful home, peaceful kids."

~ *Tuned in Parents*

"Books can teach children many things, but a story that can instill such affection in today's youth is rather amazing! That is where the Joyohboy **Love is the Moon, the Stars, and the Sky** book comes in...Do yourself, your child, your family, and the world a favor by incorporating this fantastic array of books into your own book collection."

~ Randi, *Eighty MPH Mom*

Collect all of the *Joyohboy* books!

Available on Amazon

The Joyohboy book series is part of
Peace Place for Kids

It's not about finding peace or looking for peace. It's about connecting with peace. At Peace Place, we give children the tools to connect with the place of peace. You can't strive, work hard, or study hard to find peace. Peace is a place of letting go and then the connection happens. How do children who are taught the opposite learn to let go? We let go of tension in the body through movement and exercises that move energy. We let go of thought through medita-tion. We let go of control by focusing on positive energy filled with gratitude. Why peace? Because peace is where your life soars.

Connecting with peace puts the child in harmony with life. When children connect with peace, they live a life of joy, because that is what they attract. They are able to go to that place of peace inside, no matter what is happening on the outside, and ultimately, peace is where the power lies. They are in control when they are at peace. External influences don't bother them. When children connect with peace, they are able to listen to their own inner voice and intuition. Intuition guides the children to do what is best for them, which brings them to a vibration of peace. This vibration of peace attracts more good things and takes the child round and round in a circle of joy. Join us on this mindful journey raising peaceful kids in a vibration of love.

peace place
for kids ®

facebook.com/joyohboybooks f 𝕐 twitter.com/peaceplace4kids
instagram.com/peaceplaceforkids 🄾 🅟 pinterest.com/peaceplace4kids

www.peaceplaceforkids.com

joyohboy

raising peaceful kids